DISNEY'S 101
DALMATIANS

WHAT IF
CRUELLA DE VIL WAS YOUR
LUNCH LADY?

Illustrated by Sparky Moore

DISNEY
PRESS

NEW YORK

Library of Congress Catalog Card Number: 96–84318
ISBN: 0-7868-4103-6
First Edition
1 3 5 7 9 10 8 6 4 2

Printed in the United States of America.

WHAT IF
CRUELLA DE VIL WAS YOUR
Lunch Lady

If you like, I can pop that in a doggie bag for you.

Cruella De Vil is one of a kind—
or is she? For although there *may*
be only one Cruella, there are
many de-villainesses. So look
around, you may spot Cruella-
like characters at your local play-
ground, in school, at the mall,
or perhaps, every now and then,
in your own mirror.

Will that be with or
without kibble?

One more flying brussels sprout from you and you'll be consigned to the less fashionable section of the cafeteria.

So it's burned! Black is *always* in style.

WHAT IF CRUELLA DE VIL WAS YOUR Police Officer

You'll have to pay a hefty fine—and don't let me see you mixing plaids on my beat again!

Those children wearing
Save the Rain Forest T-shirts
will have to cross at their
own risk.

We're now enforcing the *no* leash law.

WHAT IF CRUELLA DE VIL WAS YOUR Mother

Of course you may have a pet . . . temporarily.

You want me to sign a note permitting you to join Concerned Children Devoted to the Kindly Treatment of Animals? Well, I'm not sure I want you hanging out with that sort of crowd.

Go to your room—and redecorate it!

Remember, looks are *everything*. You can cultivate brains and personality in your spare time.

I have no objection to your becoming a vegetarian. I, too, have always been devoted to animals—the attractive ones, anyway.

Trust Mummy—you don't want any part of *that* preschool; several of the children were entirely without accessories.

WHAT IF CRUELLA DE VIL WAS YOUR
Sales Clerk

See, shopping is so much more fun than studying.

Your mother is just wrong, darling. Expensive clothes are always the best.

If you're going to wear a poodle skirt, wear a *poodle skirt.*

This rain forest resort wear
practically flies off the racks.
Must be the parrots.

Try our winter arctic wear—if it's good enough for polar bears, it's good enough for you.

Well, if you're going to wear something that's four sizes too big for you, at least remember to adjust accessories accordingly.

WHAT IF
CRUELLA DE VIL WAS YOUR
Gym Teacher

**Think of me
as more of
an "athletic stylist."**

Laps! I demand more laps!

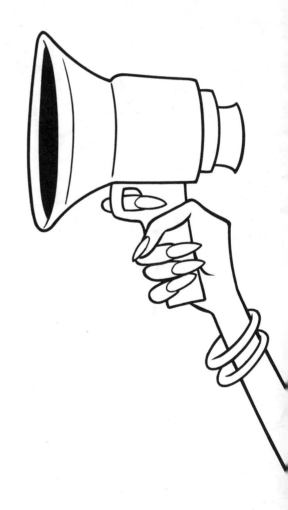

In these leather bathing
suits you'll be as sleek as
seals.

Kids today are too soft. Try running the obstacle course in high heels. Then we'll talk.

Today's sports are stalking and trapping.

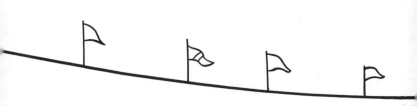

If you can't be in the game, wear something fabulous on the bench.

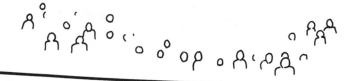

What if
Cruella De Vil Was Your
Guidance
Counselor

I can't see that talking in
class should bring you to my

office. Perhaps it was really
your outfit that was loud.

This report says you have a poor attitude—but to me it looks more like a matter of confused accessorizing.

You've indicated an interest in politics. Good choice! The world can always use more dictators.

Today's behavioral seminars are "How to Get Extra Lunch Money Without Having to Work for It" and "Getting Total Control over Your Trust Fund by Age Sixteen."

Trust me, kid—colleges will be more impressed with a really killer fashion sense than they will with grades and SAT scores.

If your parents don't see things your way, try sending *them* to *their* room.

WHAT IF
CRUELLA DE VIL WAS YOUR
Ballet Teacher

Everybody take your
positions for the Dance
of the Dobermans.

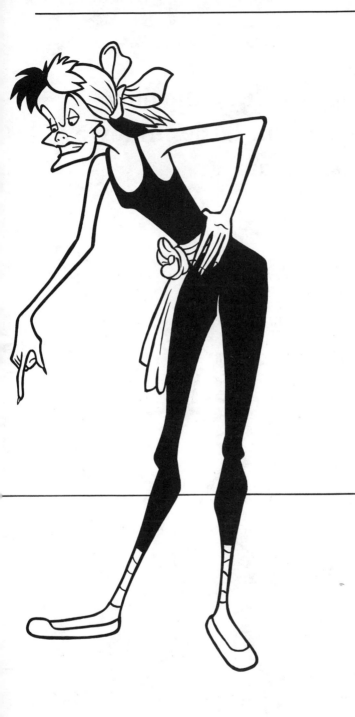

I bet you'll be the only sugarplum fairies in town wearing fur.

Six-inch heels make a much more elegant statement than those dowdy toe shoes.

Remember to watch those after-school snacks. These leotards have no secrets!

That was most definitely a
pas de *don't*!

I'm afraid some of you dancers will be playing scenery—most likely offstage as well.

WHAT IF
CRUELLA DE VIL WAS YOUR
Baby-sitter

I adore puppies . . . I
mean children. Are they
house-trained?

My fee is twenty-five dollars an hour—plus total, unlimited power.

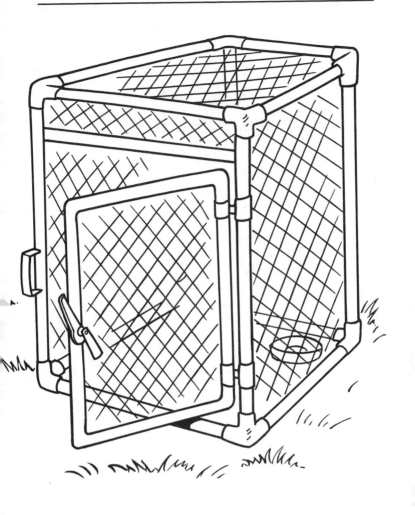

Behave, or you'll be spending
the night in the kennel.

Where I come from, *all* children wear leashes.

I honestly don't care *when* you go to sleep, but you'd better be faking it when your parents return!

If *you* change the baby, I'll let you stay up all night.

Pipe down or the muzzles
go on again.

WHAT IF
CRUELLA DE VIL WAS YOUR
Next-Door
Neighbor

DOGS
WELCOME

Drat! There's another of those pesky environmental protection agents hiding in the bushes again!

Sorry! I'm afraid this is a "pets only" open house.

I see no point in having a neighborhood patrol that refuses to report fashion violations.

Drat! I've tripped the alarm
on their doghouse again!

I wonder if I could persuade the fire department to put a few extra hydrants out in front of the house.

WHAT IF CRUELLA DE VIL WAS YOUR Scout Master

That's "Scout Mistress" to you!

Remember our troop motto: Through Winter, Rain, or Sunny Skies, Remember to Accessorize!

Today we will discuss the requirements for the Camping with Style merit badge.

Here in Troop De Vil we have our own special merit badges—Fashion Without Scruples is a personal favorite.

Why don't we just rough it in a nice four-star hotel? We can sing campfire songs in the lounge.

One can observe nature just as easily from the back of a limousine.

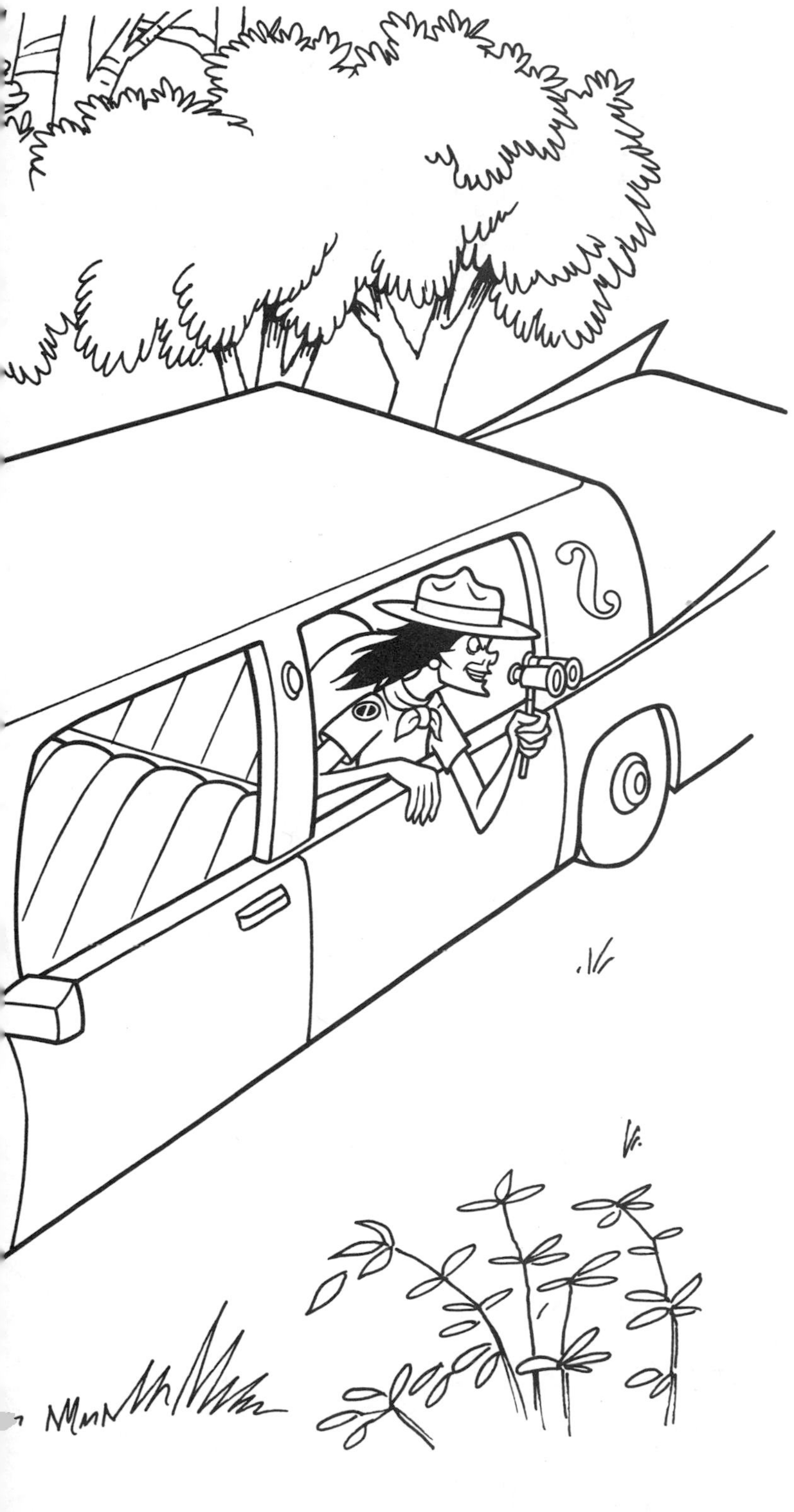

WHAT IF
CRUELLA DE VIL WAS YOUR
Art Teacher

I've already suffered for my
art—now it's your turn.

Get out your modeling clay.
And remember, one can
never have too many
ashtrays.

These paintbrushes are genuine chinchilla. Use them carefully or you'll be contributing to the increased discomfort of a number of already chilly rodents.

Yes, you're going to paint portraits of me, *again*.

Regardless of whether you possess any actual talent, a reputation for an artistic temperament can be a potent weapon.

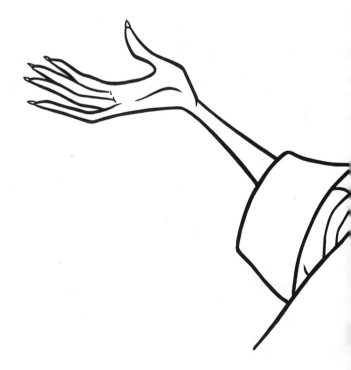

If you can't sell it, it's not
art.